HUEY, DEWEY, AND LOUIE'S CAMPFIRE SURPRISE

A Book About Time

By Bruce Isen

Illustrated by Russell Schroeder and Don Williams

A GOLDEN BOOK • NEW YORK

Western Publishing Company Inc., Racine, Wisconsin 53404

Huey, Dewey, and Louie raced into their Uncle Donald's bedroom, calling, "Uncle Donald! Uncle Donald!"

"What is it, boys?" Donald asked, waking up. He looked at his alarm clock. "It's only **seven o'clock** in the morning. There's another hour until you boys have to leave for day camp."

7:00 a.m.

"Uncle Donald," said Huey, "may we borrow your watch today?"

"*Tonight's* the big Camp Time-of-Your-Life campfire and sleepout, and we have a surprise for all the campers at **seven o'clock**," said Dewey.

"And we have to know when it's seven!" Louie added.

"All right, all right, boys," said Donald.

Huey, Dewey, and Louie ate breakfast. Then they had
to get their gear together for the big sleepout. Each boy
had a bedroll and a knapsack with everything he'd
need. They each had something special to pack, too.

"Don't forget your costumes," Huey reminded his
brothers. "We'll need them for the campfire surprise."

"Yeah," added Dewey. "Nobody will be expecting us
to act out 'The Legend of Haunted Cave.'"

8:00 a.m.

"Uncle Mickey said we'll be stopping at Haunted Cave on our hike," said Louie. "They say the ghost of Tick-Tock Tootsie, the famous clock robber, haunts the cave."

"I heard his treasure is buried there, too," said Huey. Then he looked at the watch. **"Eight o'clock!"** he called.

"Here's the camp bus," announced Dewey as the bus driver drove the bus up and blew the horn.

The boys arrived at camp and went to flag-raising with the rest of their group. Then their counselor, Mickey Mouse, gathered the campers together and handed each one a slip of paper.

"Today is special," Mickey reminded them. "This piece of paper is our schedule for the day. We have to start our hike up Baldy Mountain on time to get to our campsite before dark."

Huey, Dewey, and Louie looked at their schedules as Mickey read one aloud.

"There it is, Haunted Cave," said Huey, pointing to his schedule. "I wonder if there really is a ghost and a treasure in there."

"Wait and see," said Mickey.

9:00—swimming
10:00—archery
11:00—arts and crafts
12:00—lunch
1:00—naptime
2:00—start hike up
Baldy Mountain
3:00—snacktime
4:00—explore Haunted Cave
5:00—pitch camp
6:00—dinner
7:00—campfire surprise
8:00—bedtime

9:00 a.m.

Dewey looked at Donald's watch. **"Nine o'clock,"** he said.

"Time for swimming," said Louie. "Let's go!"

They raced off to change into their swimming trunks, remembering to put Donald's watch in a safe, dry place before they went into the water.

They had a good swim and were soon dry and dressed again.

10:00 a.m.

"What time is it now?" asked Dewey.
"Ten o'clock," said Huey, reading Donald's watch.
"Archery!" cried Louie, reading from the schedule.
The campers ran to the archery range with Mickey.
"I got an arrow in the big red circle," said Huey.
"Bull's-eye! I hit the small black circle," said Dewey.

"Now it's **eleven o'clock**," said Louie.
"Time for arts and crafts," said Dewey. "My favorite!"
Mickey led the group to the crafts shed.
"I can't wait to get to Haunted Cave and see if there really is a ghost and a treasure," Huey said as he worked on a clay sculpture of Pluto. "How long until we get there?"

11:00 a.m.

"Well, it's **eleven o'clock** now," said Dewey. "And our schedule says we get to Haunted Cave at four o'clock." He did some quick figuring. "In one hour it will be twelve noon. Then one o'clock, two o'clock, three o'clock, four o'clock. Five hours in total!" he groaned.

Huey continued to mold his clay statue of Pluto, but he was so excited, he could hardly wait for it to be done.

12:00 noon

It was almost time to eat lunch, so Huey quickly finished his statue of Pluto as Dewey announced, **"Twelve noon.** Lunchtime!"

The group raced to the lunchroom, where their favorite lunch was waiting—cowboy stew!

1:00 p.m.

After lunch came naptime.

"Only **one o'clock**," said Huey, looking at the watch. "I don't know how I'm going to be able to have quiet time when a ghost and a treasure may be waiting up at Haunted Cave."

"Just lie down quietly," said Mickey. The boys had had such a busy morning and such a big lunch that they fell asleep in the cool shade right away.

2:00 p.m.

Everyone had a good rest. Before they knew it,
Mickey was shaking them awake again.

Huey looked at the watch. "It's **two o'clock**!" he cried.
"Time to start our hike up Baldy Mountain!"

The campers picked up their bedrolls and slung their
knapsacks on their backs.

3:00 p.m.

They hiked and hiked in the hot sun. They were glad when Mickey looked at his watch and sang out, **"Three o'clock!** Snacktime!"

Mickey passed around cookies and lemonade.

"Now let's sit and rest for a few minutes," said Mickey. "Then we'll climb a little farther and be at Haunted Cave."

"Hurray!" cried the campers.

Up at Haunted Cave, three skulking figures heard the campers' cheer. They were Big Ben and his gang of robbers.

"We know that this is where Tick-Tock Tootsie buried his loot," said Big Ben.

"But how are we going to dig it up with a bunch of pesky kids around?" asked Hickory, one of his gang.

Big Ben thought. "I have an idea," he said.

4:00 p.m.

Soon the campers were outside Haunted Cave. Dewey looked at the watch.

"**Four o'clock** on the dot!" Huey said.

"I'll go on up to our campsite and start setting up camp," said Mickey. "You boys go ahead and explore."

"Hey, look," said Dewey when the campers were inside the cave. "A big hole, and picks and shovels all ready for digging. Maybe the ghost's treasure *is* buried here!"

All the boys took turns digging. Just when their shovels hit something that sounded like a hard metal box, an eerie voice cried, "Whooooo dares disturb my looooot?"

5:00 p.m.

"It's a ghost," all the boys shouted.

"Uncle Mickey says there are no such things as ghosts," said Louie. But the boys were afraid anyway. They ran the rest of the way up Baldy Mountain.

"What happened, boys?" asked Mickey, surprised to see them arrive all out of breath.

"There was a ghost!" cried Huey.

Mickey chuckled. "You probably imagined it," he said.

Huey looked at the watch. "Well," he said. "It's **five o'clock**. We're still right on schedule."

The shaking boys started to pitch their tents.

Meanwhile, Big Ben and his gang were pulling up Tick-Tock Tootsie's loot.

"Heh, heh," Big Ben chuckled. "Just like we planned. They did all the work, and we got all the treasure."

"But we'd better wait till after dark to take it down the mountain," said Hickory. "We don't want to run into anybody."

6:00 p.m.

After all their exercise and the big scare, the campers were hungry for dinner. "It's **six o'clock,**" said Huey. "Let's eat!"

Mickey handed out hot dogs and buns. Each boy cleaned a stick, put the hot dog on the end, and roasted it over the open campfire. They also had baked beans, potato chips, and punch. "Mmmmm," they said as they ate.

7:00 p.m.

After cleanup, all the campers gathered around the campfire once again.

"Uncle Mickey," Huey whispered, "it's **seven o'clock**. We're going down the mountain to get dressed for our surprise. I just hope we don't meet any real ghosts!"

"There are no ghosts," Mickey repeated. To the rest of the group he said, "All right. Let's start with some songs."

In the meantime, the robbers were getting ready to leave Haunted Cave.

"It's dark enough now, boys," said Big Ben. "Let's go!" They hoisted the chest and started out of the cave.

Huey, Dewey, and Louie had put on their ghost costumes. They were trying to find the way back to the campfire.

"This way," said Huey.

"No, this way," said Dewey.

"Aaaaah!" screamed Louie when he saw strange shadows coming out of Haunted Cave.

"AAAAAH!" screamed Big Ben and his gang when they saw three ghosts in the dark. They dropped the loot and ran.

When the boys realized what had happened, they started to laugh.

"Well," said Huey, "I guess we scared away those three robbers. Now we can act out our own 'Legend of Haunted Cave' at the campfire."

"And the surprise will be this chest," said Dewey. The three boys dragged it back to the campsite.

Everyone enjoyed watching Huey, Dewey, and Louie play all the parts in their adventure at Haunted Cave. "I always said there were no ghosts," said Mickey.

At the end of the show, Dewey announced, "And now for the big surprise—Tick-Tock Tootsie's treasure!"

Louie flung open the chest. Inside were fancy old clocks and a pile of old-fashioned pocket watches.

8:00 p.m.

"There are enough treasures for everbody," said
Huey. "All we need to do is wind them up."

They set the clocks and watches, then sat and listened
to the happy ticking.

Soon the biggest clock chimed. Each boy looked at his
timepiece. They all sang out together, **"Eight o'clock!
Bedtime!"**

And the happy campers went to sleep under the stars.